Dear Parents:

Congratulations! Your child is taking the first steps on an exciting journey. The destination? Independent reading!

STEP INTO READING® will help your child get there. The program offers five steps to reading success. Each step includes fun stories and colorful art or photographs. In addition to original fiction and books with favorite characters, there are Step into Reading Non-Fiction Readers, Phonics Readers and Boxed Sets, Sticker Readers, and Comic Readers—a complete literacy program with something to interest every child.

Learning to Read, Step by Step!

Ready to Read   Preschool–Kindergarten
• big type and easy words • rhyme and rhythm • picture clues
For children who know the alphabet and are eager to begin reading.

Reading with Help   Preschool–Grade 1
• basic vocabulary • short sentences • simple stories
For children who recognize familiar words and sound out new words with help.

Reading on Your Own   Grades 1–3
• engaging characters • easy-to-follow plots • popular topics
For children who are ready to read on their own.

Reading Paragraphs   Grades 2–3
• challenging vocabulary • short paragraphs • exciting stories
For newly independent readers who read simple sentences with confidence.

Ready for Chapters   Grades 2–4
• chapters • longer paragraphs • full-color art
For children who want to take the plunge into chapter books but still like colorful pictures.

STEP INTO READING® is designed to give every child a successful reading experience. The grade levels are only guides; children will progress through the steps at their own speed, developing confidence in their reading.

Remember, a lifetime love of reading starts with a single step!

Copyright © 2019 Disney Enterprises, Inc. All rights reserved. Published in the United States by Random House Children's Books, a division of Penguin Random House LLC, 1745 Broadway, New York, NY 10019, and in Canada by Penguin Random House Canada Limited, Toronto, in conjunction with Disney Enterprises, Inc.

Step into Reading, Random House, and the Random House colophon are registered trademarks of Penguin Random House LLC.

Visit us on the Web!
StepIntoReading.com
rhcbooks.com

Educators and librarians, for a variety of teaching tools, visit us at RHTeachersLibrarians.com

ISBN 978-0-7364-3991-6 (trade) — ISBN 978-0-7364-8279-0 (lib. bdg.)
— ISBN 978-0-7364-3992-3 (ebook)

Printed in the United States of America   10 9 8 7 6 5 4 3 2

DISNEY

M⊚ANA

Moana's
New Friend

adapted by Jennifer Liberts
based on an original story by Suzanne Francis
illustrated by the Disney Storybook Art Team

Random House 🏠 New York

Moana loves

the ocean!

She loves

to ride the waves

with her pal Pua.

One day,
Moana and Pua meet
a friendly sea turtle.

The sea turtle smiles.

Moana says hello.

The sea turtle loves
to surf!
She stays and plays
all day.

Moana names
her new friend Lolo.
Moana and Pua
say goodbye to Lolo.

Lolo comes back

to play every day.

The friends have fun.
They play games, swim,
and surf.

One night,
Moana and Gramma Tala
look for seashells
on the beach.

Moana sees Lolo crawl
onto the sand.
Lolo digs a hole
by a coconut tree.

Lolo lays eggs in a nest.
There are baby turtles
inside!

When the eggs hatch,
the babies will go
to the ocean.

Each day,

Moana checks the nest.

She hopes to see

the baby turtles hatch.

A big storm comes.

Moana and Pua run home.

The trees bend and sway

in the strong wind.

After the storm,

Moana goes to the beach.

A tree has fallen

on top of the nest!

The turtle eggs
are trapped!
Moana asks her friends
for help.

Moana and her friends
work hard.
Together they move
the tree.

The next day,
the eggs hatch.
The baby turtles
crawl out!

They crawl
to the ocean.
Moana and her friends
protect them.

Moana gives them shade.

Pua chases away a bird.

The baby turtles get
to the water safely!

Moana is so proud!
Lolo's babies are all safe.
They swim and play
in Moana and Lolo's
favorite place—the ocean!